TYLER PERRY

Joanne Mattern

Mitchell Lane
PUBLISHERS

P.O. Box 196
Hockessin, Delaware 19707
Visit us on the web: www.mitchelllane.com
Comments? Email us: mitchelllane@mitchelllane.com

Mitchell Lane
PUBLISHERS

Printing   1   2   3   4   5   6   7   8   9

A Robbie Reader Biography

Aaron Rodgers	Drake Bell & Josh Peck	LeBron James
Abigail Breslin	Dr. Seuss	Mia Hamm
Adrian Peterson	Dwayne "The Rock" Johnson	Michael Strahan
Albert Einstein	Dwyane Wade	Miley Cyrus
Albert Pujols	Dylan & Cole Sprouse	Miranda Cosgrove
Alex Rodriguez	Eli Manning	Philo Farnsworth
Aly and AJ	Emily Osment	Raven-Symoné
Amanda Bynes	Emma Watson	Roy Halladay
AnnaSophia Robb	Hilary Duff	Selena Gomez
Ashley Tisdale	Jaden Smith	Shaquille O'Neal
Brenda Song	Jamie Lynn Spears	Story of Harley-Davidson
Brittany Murphy	Jennette McCurdy	Sue Bird
Carmelo Anthony	Jeremy Lin	Syd Hoff
Charles Schulz	Jesse McCartney	Taylor Lautner
Chris Johnson	Jimmie Johnson	Tiki Barber
Cliff Lee	Johnny Gruelle	Tim Lincecum
Dakota Fanning	Jonas Brothers	Tom Brady
Dale Earnhardt Jr.	Jordin Sparks	Tony Hawk
David Archuleta	Justin Beiber	Troy Polamalu
Debby Ryan	Keke Palmer	Tyler Perry
Demi Lovato	Larry Fitzgerald	Victoria Justice
Donovan McNabb		

Library of Congress Cataloging-in-Publication Data
Mattern, Joanne, 1963–
  Tyler Perry / by Joanne Mattern.
      p. cm. — (A Robbie reader)
  Includes bibliographical references and index.
  ISBN 978-1-61228-334-0 (library bound)
  1. Perry, Tyler—Juvenile literature. 2. Authors, American—20th century—Biography—Juvenile literature. 3. African American authors—Biography—Juvenile literature. 4. Actors—United States—Biography—Juvenile literature. 5. Motion picture producers and directors—United States—Biography—Juvenile literature. 6. Television producers and directors—United States—Biography—Juvenile literature. I. Title.
  PS3616.E795Z63 2012
  812'.6—dc23
  [B]
                                                                                    2012018309
eBook ISBN: 9781612284026

ABOUT THE AUTHOR: Joanne Mattern is the author of more than 200 nonfiction books for young readers. Her books for Mitchell Lane include biographies of such notables as Michelle Obama, Benny Goodman, Blake Lively, Selena, LeBron James, and Peyton Manning. Mattern lives in New York State with her husband, four children, and an assortment of pets.

TABLE OF CONTENTS

Words in **bold** type can be found in the glossary.

Tyler Perry has become one of Hollywood's most successful and well-known producers and actors. His ground-breaking plays and movies introduced people around the world to his opinionated character, Madea.

A Second Chance

Tyler Perry was excited. But he was also scared. It was 1998, and 28-year-old Perry was about to take a big chance. He was putting on a musical play in the city of Atlanta.

This was not the first time Tyler had tried to impress an audience. In 1992, he had put on the same show, called *I Know I've Been Changed.* Tyler wrote the show about things he had experienced in his own life, and tied in a powerful Christian message. It asked the audience to forgive people who had hurt them in their lives. Tyler put all the money he had into the play. He rented a theater and hired actors. He was hoping to attract a large audience.

CHAPTER ONE

Tyler Perry and Cicely Tyson at the Broadway opening of the play
The Color Purple. Tyson is one of the most respected and beloved
African-American actresses and has appeared in several of Tyler Perry's
movies.

Thirty people came to see Tyler's play. **Critics** did not like it. The show closed in one weekend, and Tyler lost all his money. But even though he was broke and he had nowhere to live, Tyler did not give up.

For six years, Tyler worked on *I Know I've Been Changed*, rewriting the entire show. He made it better and better, and he continued showing it in the Christian community. Finally, in 1998, Tyler got another chance. A theater owner offered him a **contract** for the show. Tyler was ready to try again.

People started coming to see the show. Critics gave the show great reviews. Before long, the musical was sold out every night, and Tyler had to move the show to a larger theater. *I Know I've Been Changed* was a big **success**!

Tyler Perry always believed in himself. He did not give up when his show failed the first time. Tyler's confidence and belief in himself and God would lead him to an amazing career as an actor, writer, and director.

Tyler Perry's mother, Willie Maxine, was a loving and protective force throughout his childhood. Perry modeled the character of Madea after his mother and other female relatives.

Rough Beginnings

Emmitt Perry, Jr. was born on September 13, 1969, in New Orleans, Louisiana. His mother, Willie Maxine Perry, was a preschool teacher, and his father, Emmitt Perry, Sr., worked as a carpenter. There were four children in the Perry household.

Emmitt was close to his mother, but he and his father did not get along. His father often beat Emmitt and other members of the family. Emmitt once told *JET* magazine that his father's "answer to everything was to beat it out of you." When he was sixteen years old, Emmitt changed his first name to Tyler. He did not want to have the same name as his father.

Tyler's mother tried to protect him from the violence at home. To do this, Mrs. Perry took Tyler with her everywhere so he would not have to stay home with his father. Tyler spent a lot of time with his mother at the local beauty parlor. He listened to the women there talking to each other and sharing stories. Later, Tyler would use those memories to create the characters and stories in his movies.

Tyler and his family went to church every week. He found strength in his belief in God, and he loved how kind the people there were to each other. Tyler enjoyed attending church events. Church was a place where he felt safe.

But when Tyler was a teenager, he felt lost and alone. He was angry because of how he was treated at home, and his anger got him kicked out of high school. He did return to earn a general diploma later on. Tyler did not like living at home, and he felt sad and upset all the time. Tyler had to find a way out of his situation. That way out was writing.

When Tyler was about twenty years old, he was watching *The Oprah Winfrey Show.*

Media giant Oprah Winfrey is one of Tyler Perry's biggest fans. Here they appear together at the Los Angeles premiere of the movie *Precious*, a brutally honest look at one teenager's rise from an abusive home.

Oprah told viewers that writing down their feelings could help make them feel better. Tyler took Oprah's advice, and began writing a series of letters to himself. Tyler wrote about his feelings and his problems, using made up names so no one would know he was writing about himself. He soon discovered that he loved writing. Tyler had found a way to make his life better.

Tyler Perry is also a best-selling author. His 2006 book, *Don't Make a Black Woman Take Off Her Earrings* provides humor, wisdom, and advice from Perry's well-known character, Madea. Here Perry appears at a book signing in New York City.

Meet Madea

In 1990, Tyler Perry moved to Atlanta. He worked at different jobs to earn money, but his heart was really in his writing. Tyler used the series of letters he had written to himself to write *I Know I've Been Changed.*

By 1992, Tyler had saved up $12,000, and he put all of it into his play. Tyler directed, **produced**, and starred in the show. But after the show failed, Tyler found himself living in his car. This was not easy, considering his size. "Can you imagine a six-foot-five man sleeping in a Geo Metro?" he joked in an interview with *Essence* magazine.

Tyler kept working on his show and finally turned it into one that audiences loved. After his success in 1998 with *I Know I've Been Changed*, Tyler decided to write and produce other plays.

In 2000, Tyler wrote a play called *I Can Do Bad All By Myself*. The play starred a character named Madea, a strong African-American woman who says what she thinks. "Madea is a cross between my mother and my aunt. She's the type of grandmother that was on every corner when I was growing up," Tyler told a reporter from *60 Minutes*. But Tyler didn't just create the character of Madea, he played her as well. He put on makeup and wore women's clothes to bring Madea to life onstage.

Tyler traveled all over the South performing his plays for audiences that were mostly African-American. In 2005, *Forbes* magazine reported that he had sold more than $100 million in tickets. The magazine also said that "the 300 live shows he produces each year are attended by an average of 35,000 people a week."

Tyler Perry was a huge star in the African-American theater world. But it was time to take

Madea has become one of the most beloved and well-known characters in African-American movies and helps Perry spread his message of love, family, and belief in God.

Madea and his other characters to the big screen. Soon, Tyler would be a star all over the United States.

Perry at the premiere of *Diary of a Mad Black Woman*, his first movie.

Fame and Controversy

In 2005, Tyler Perry produced and starred in his first movie. The movie was called *Diary of a Mad Black Woman*. Like his plays, the movie featured Tyler playing Madea. Tyler spent $5 million to make the movie, and it earned more than fifty million dollars at the box office in the United States. Tyler and Madea were a big hit!

Not long after Tyler released his first movie, Madea was back on the big screen. In 2006, Tyler released *Madea's Family Reunion*. The

film made more than thirty million dollars its first weekend and was the number one movie at the box office.

The year 2006 brought more than just big screen success for Tyler—he also made his television debut with *Tyler Perry's House of Payne*. The show is about an African-American family of different **generations** living together. *House of Payne* became very popular and continued to air for many years.

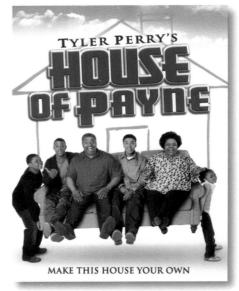

His second television show, *Meet the Browns*, followed the adventures of the Brown family, who managed a home for seniors. It ran from 2009 until 2011.

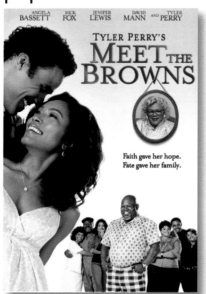

Tyler continued to make movies featuring the character of Madea.

Perry poses as Madea in the movie *Madea's Big Happy Family*. Perry first played the part of Madea onstage and continues to portray his most popular character in movies.

In 2009, Tyler released *Madea Goes to Jail*, and followed up with *I Can Do Bad All by Myself*. Both movies opened at number one at the box office.

Despite her sensible, old-fashioned appearance, Madea always seems to get into trouble. Perry poses with a poster of Madea at the premiere of *Madea Goes to Jail* in 2009.

Although Tyler Perry has a huge fan base, not everyone loves his work. Many critics say Madea is a **stereotype** and is not a good image of an African-American woman. Some critics say they especially dislike Tyler promoting these stereotypes, since he is African-American himself. Tyler was upset by these comments because Madea and his other characters are

Perry poses with the cast of *I Can Do Bad All By Myself*, including Mary J. Blige, Kwesi Boakye, Taraji P. Henson, and Freddy Siglar at the movie's New York City premiere in 2009.

based on people he knew. He told *60 Minutes*, "It is so insulting. It's attitudes like that, that make Hollywood think that these people do not exist." Tyler said that when people come to his movies to see Madea, it allows him to spread his message of "God, love, faith, forgiveness, family."

One of Tyler's greatest fans is Oprah Winfrey. Oprah told *60 Minutes*, "I think he grew up being raised by strong, black women. And so much of what he does is really in celebration of that."

Perry and actress Tessa Thompson pose together at a special 2010 showing of *For Colored Girls*, one of the rare Perry movies that he did not appear in.

Reaching Out

Madea may be Tyler Perry's most famous character, but he is known for other movies too. In 2009, he and Oprah Winfrey produced and provided **financial** support for the movie *Precious*. *Precious* told the dramatic story of an abused and homeless African-American teenager. The movie not only won two Academy Awards, but it also allowed Tyler to show the world how much children suffer when they are abused.

Tyler also wrote, produced, and directed several movies that he did not appear in. These movies include *Daddy's Little Girls* and *For Colored Girls*. Like his other projects, these movies focus on African-American characters and their struggles and triumphs.

Tyler Perry directed many notable performers in *Daddy's Little Girls*. Here he poses with Tracee Ellis Ross, Gabrielle Union, Idris Elba, and other members of the cast at the movie's premiere in Hollywood in 2007.

In 2006, Tyler opened a movie studio in Atlanta, and in 2008 moved the studio to its current location. Tyler's studio includes five sound stages, a **post-production** unit, a theater, and areas for hosting **media** events. This studio is the heart of Tyler's business **empire**, which has brought many jobs and positive media attention to Atlanta. It also provides Tyler a place to create his television shows on a fast-paced schedule. "It takes a week to do a **sitcom** in Hollywood," he told *The Telegraph*. "I do a show a day in my studio, three or four shows a week."

Tyler donates much of his time and money to charity. He supports many charities that help the homeless, including Feeding America, Covenant House, Hosea Feed the Hungry, and Project Adventure. He built a community called Perry Place for people who lost their homes in New Orleans during Hurricane Katrina. Tyler has also built several churches. In 2010, he

Perry is always happy to raise money for charity. In 2011, Perry helped out during an auction to benefit charity: water, which brings clean water to communities around the world. The charity's founder, Scott Harrison, happily hugged Perry onstage to thank him for his support.

Perry has won many awards for his professional work as well as his projects to benefit African Americans and other people around the world. Here he accepts the Chairman Award at the NAACP Image Awards in Los Angeles in 2010.

donated $1 million to help earthquake victims in Haiti.

In 2009, Tyler read about a group of 65 children in Philadelphia who had been banned from a local swim club because they were African-American. Tyler paid for all the children to go on a trip to Walt Disney World. He wrote on his web site, "I want them to know that for every act of evil that a few people will throw at you, there are millions more who will do something kind for them."

Tyler's work has also brought him many awards. He has won several awards including a BET Comedy Award, Black Movie Award, Black Reel Award, and two NAACP Image Awards.

Tyler Perry has achieved great things in his life. He never stopped believing in himself and in God, and kept going when times were hard. Now, through humor and entertainment, Tyler Perry is showing the world just how important family, love, and laughter really are.

CHRONOLOGY

1969   Emmitt Perry, Jr. born on September 13 in New Orleans, Louisiana.

1985   Changes his name to Tyler Perry.

1990   Moves to Atlanta, Georgia.

1992   Writes and performs in *I Know I've Been Changed*, which closes after its first weekend.

1998   Puts on a successful new production of *I Know I've Been Changed*.

2000   Introduces the character of Madea in his play, *I Can Do Bad All By Myself*.

2005   Makes his first movie, *Diary of a Mad Black Woman*.

2006   Writes, produces, directs, and stars in *Madea's Family Reunion*; his first television show, *Tyler Perry's House of Payne*, debuts.

2007   Writes, directs, and produces *Daddy's Little Girls*.

2009   With Oprah Winfrey, becomes executive producer of *Precious*.

2012   Stars in the title role of *I, Alex Cross*.

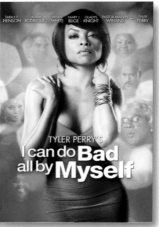

FILMOGRAPHY

2005 *Diary of a Mad Black Woman*
2006 *Madea's Family Reunion*
2007 *Daddy's Little Girls*
      Why Did I Get Married?
2008 *Meet the Browns*
      The Family That Preys
2009 *Star Trek*
      I Can Do Bad All by Myself

2009 *Madea Goes to Jail*
      Precious
2010 *Why Did I Get Married Too?*
      For Colored Girls
2011 *Madea's Big Happy Family*
2012 *Good Deeds*
      I, Alex Cross
      Madea's Witness Protection
      The Marriage Counselor

TELEVISION

2006-2012   *Tyler Perry's House of Payne*
2009-2011   *Meet the Browns*
2011-present *Tyler Perry's For Better or Worse*

FIND OUT MORE

Books

Uschan, Michael V. *Tyler Perry.* Farmington Hills, Michigan: Lucent Books, 2010.

Works Consulted

"About Tyler." TylerPerry.com, 2012.
http://www.tylerperry.com/biography

Christian, Margena A. "Tyler Perry: Meet the man behind the urban theater character Madea." *JET,* December 1, 2003.

Garratt, Sheryl. "Interview: Tyler Perry, movie mogul." *The Telegraph,* August 21, 2010.
http://www.telegraph.co.uk/culture/film/7956763/
Interview-Tyler-Perry-movie-mogul.html

Johnson, Pamela K. "Diary of a Brilliant Black Man." *Essence,* February 16, 2006. http://www.essence.com/2006/02/16/
diary-of-a-brilliant-black-man/

Pulley, Brett. "A Showbiz Whiz." *Forbes,* September 15, 2005.
http://www.forbes.com/forbes/2005/1003/
075.html

"Tyler Perry." Biography.com, 2012.
http://www.biography.com/print/profile/tyler-perry-361274

"Tyler Perry's Amazing Journey to the Top." *60 Minutes,* October 22, 2009. http://www.cbsnews.com/
stories/2009/10/22/60minutes/main5410095.shtml

Winfrey, Oprah. "Oprah Talks to Tyler Perry." *O, The Oprah Magazine,* December 2010. http://www.oprah.com/
entertainment/Oprah-Interviews-Tyler-Perry_1/1

On the Internet

Official Tyler Perry Web Site
http://www.tylerperry.com/

Tyler Perry Bio: KidzWorld.com
http://www.kidzworld.com/article/25488-tyler-perry-bio

Tyler Perry: ImdB
http://www.imdb.com/name/nm1347153/bio

GLOSSARY

contract (KON-trakt)—A legal agreement between people or companies.

critics (KRIT-iks)—People who review books, movies, plays, or television shows.

empire (EM-pahy-er)—A large group of companies controlled by one person or group of people.

financial (fi-NAN-shuhl)—Related to money.

generation (jen-uh-RAY-shuhn)—All of the people born around the same time.

media (MEE-dee-uh)—Television, movies, magazines, web sites, and other methods of making information available to people.

post-production (POST pruh-DUK-shuhn)—Work on a movie after it is filmed, such as editing or adding music or sound effects.

produced (pruh-DOOSED)—Made a movie, television program, or music recording.

sitcom (SIT-kom)—Situation comedy; a television show that finds humor in ordinary life.

stereotype (STAIR-ee-uh-tahyp)—An incorrect idea or image about a particular group of people.

success (SUK-sess)—Something that is done well, and has a good outcome.

INDEX